About the Author

Stephanie Baudet was born in Cheshire, England, and grew up in Australia and New Zealand. After training as a nurse, she returned to England and now lives in Buckinghamshire with her husband and two cats. She has a grown-up daughter who lives in Australia. She has also written *A Present From Egypt, Double Bubble Trouble and Someone Else's Shoes* for Poolbeg.

Website: www.stephaniebaudet.co.uk
Author of 13 books including 'The Incredible Shrinking Hippo' (Puffin). 4 more coming out in next 2 years.

Also by Stephanie Baudet

For Emily Jane,

the latest member of the Cleghorn Clan

It was while they were having spelling that it happened.

Mrs Ronson was writing on the blackboard. The classroom door was slightly open.

Something in the doorway attracted Paul's attention and he gasped. A little white feathery head was peeping through. A little white feathery head with a brown beak. It was his pet hen, Milly. She must have followed him to school!

Someone giggled. Someone squealed. "Quiet, please," said the teacher.

The little white feathery head came further into the room followed by the rest of Milly. She stood looking round, her head jerking this way and that, making her red floppy comb wobble about. Then she saw Paul and came towards him, her little feet making a tap-tapping noise on the floor.

More giggles broke out and Mrs Ronson turned round.

"What is the matter?" she asked. She didn't see Milly sitting under Paul's chair and no one told her either. She turned back to the board.

Milly came out from under Paul's chair and tap-tapped her way to the front of the classroom. Then, in a flurry of wings, she

flew up onto the teacher's desk and settled comfortably on top of the spelling books in the wire tray.

The whole class burst into laughter and Mrs Ronson turned round, frowning.

Then she saw Milly and jumped back, dropping the chalk in fright. "Where has it come from?" she asked.

Paul put up his hand. "It's my hen, Milly. She follows me everywhere."

Everyone knew that Paul lived only three doors from the school.

Mrs Ronson smiled. "Well, she can stay until break and then you'd better take her home, Paul. In the meantime, we'll find a box for her. She can't sit on the spelling."

She lifted Milly out of the tray and put her into a cardboard box. "What's this?" she asked, holding up something smooth and white. Milly had laid an egg!

When the bell went for break, Paul lifted up Milly and tucked her under one arm while he opened the door. In that

instant, the hen struggled free, fluttered to the ground and sprinted off along the corridor. Then she disappeared through a doorway.

It was the head teacher's office!

Paul knocked on the slightly open door. There was no reply so he pushed it open. Mrs Davis, the head teacher, was not there. Neither was Milly.

Paul stood still, wondering what to do. He listened hard. There was no tap-tapping of little feet or scuffles of a nosy little beak rummaging into things.

Just silence.

"Have you come to see me, Paul?" said a voice behind him.

Paul jumped. "No, Mrs Davis. I'm looking for Milly."

"Milly?" said Mrs Davis, frowning. "I don't know anyone called Milly. Is she a new girl?"

"She's a hen," said Paul. "She followed me to school and now I can't find her."

"I see," said Mrs Davis. "Well, she can't be far. I'll keep an eye out for her."

But for the rest of the morning there was no sign of Milly.

"Maybe she's gone home," said Jenny Tucker.

"We can organise a search party after dinner," said Ian Baker.

The usual clatter and babble of the dining-room died down as Mrs Davis came in, now wearing her grey jacket and looking worried. She held up her hand for silence.

"I seem to have lost my car keys," she said. "Could everyone please look out for them?"

Milly's lost too, thought Paul, and she's more important than a bunch of keys.

As Mrs Davis turned towards the counter, there, stuck to the back of her jacket, was a white feather. So Milly *had* been in her office and poking around her jacket too. Could she possibly have had anything to do with the missing keys?

"I've found them!" cried a voice. It was Mrs Brown, the dinner lady. "Your keys, Mrs Davis. They're in the rice pudding!"

She lifted the ladle out of the big pot and then carefully picked something out with her fingers. Creamy, lumpy pudding slid off the bunch of keys and sploshed onto the counter.

The dining-room was in an uproar.
Teachers scowled accusingly at the
children and the children laughed,
especially Paul's class who guessed the
truth.

Then there was a piercing shriek from
the kitchen, followed by a loud cackle. To
everyone's surprise, Mrs Brown dashed

out of the kitchen and stood, holding her skirt tightly round her legs, hopping from one foot to the other in a strange sort of dance.

"There's something in the cupboard!" she squeaked.

Mrs Ronson got up from her chair and walked calmly into the kitchen. She, too, had guessed who the culprit was.

There was a squawking sound and Milly skittered out of the kitchen, wings flapping, pursued by Mrs Ronson. The two of them disappeared out into the corridor amidst cheers from their audience.

But Milly was too quick. She was enjoying her adventures at school and was not going to be caught. Mrs Ronson came back without her, shaking her head.

"Please make sure, in future, that Milly is shut in the hen house when you come to school," she said to Paul. "She's gone outside. I hope she's gone home."

Milly had not gone home, and all the running about had made her thirsty. She was busy having a drink of water out of the caretaker's watering can when he saw

her. Water that he'd prepared for the big tubs of flowers at the school entrance. Water, he told Paul's class, that had some special stuff in it to feed the flowers. It was called SUPERGROW. It made flowers grow quicker and bigger but he didn't know what effect it would have on a hen.

"It might make her grow," said Paul.

"As big as a horse," said Jenny Tucker.

"As big as an elephant," said Ian Baker.

"Oh, I don't think so," said Mrs Ronson.

But all afternoon Paul thought about Milly growing bigger . . . and bigger . . . and bigger.

The classroom went suddenly dark and he thought it must be giant Milly walking past the window.

But it was only a thundercloud.

After school, as he walked along the footpath, he saw a huge white feather lying on the ground and picked it up. This *must* be Milly's feather. But where had she gone?

He ran in through his gate and round the back to the small hen house. It was empty. It would be too small for Milly now, wouldn't it?

"I haven't seen her all day," said Mum, looking worried.

"She came to school," said Paul. "She laid an egg on the spelling books and put

Mrs Davis's car keys into the rice pudding and gave Mrs Brown a fright."

He didn't tell her about the SUPERGROW. He didn't want Mum to worry.

"But where is she now?" asked Mum.

"She ran away," said Paul, "and no one could catch her."

"I expect she'll find her way home," said Mum.

Paul wasn't sure he wanted her back now. Not giant Milly. Dad would have to build a much bigger hen house and her giant feet would make an awful mess of the garden when she scratched. Her clucks and cackles would be CLUCKS and CACKLES, mega-loud, and they'd have to block their ears.

And what about her eggs! They'd be so big that Mrs Brown would be able to make scrambled eggs for the whole school from just one egg.

When Paul finally got to sleep he dreamed of Milly, as tall as a building, and people running in fear of being crushed by her huge feet.

The next morning Mum smiled and said, "She's back."

Paul went out to have a look. The hen-house door was firmly closed and he peered in through the wire mesh. Milly sat quietly on her perch, dozing. Ordinary Milly. Normal-sized Milly.

Had she ever been a giant hen? Had the effect of the SUPERGROW worn off? Or had he imagined it all and she'd stayed her normal size all along? Paul wasn't sure. And what about the feather?

When he got to school he showed it to Mrs Ronson who took out a big book about birds and opened a page showing lots of different feathers.

"Well," she said. "It's a stork's feather. They're very rare in England now."

Paul nodded, disappointed, twirling the feather between his fingers.

Suddenly Ian Baker rushed into the classroom followed by several others. He was out of breath.

"What is it, Ian?" asked Mrs Ronson.

Ian's face was pale and he took a deep breath. "Our big wheat field," he said.

"The wheat was ripe and ready for harvesting but now it's gone. Only the stalks are left and there are some really weird footprints on the ground. Dad says he can't imagine who or what has done it."

Paul smiled to himself. He could.